ALBERT AND THE BLUBBER MONSTER

LUKE TEMPLE
ILLUSTRATED

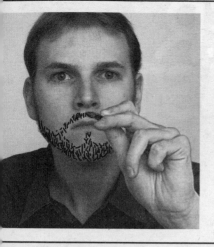

Luke Temple was born on Halloween, 1988. As a child, Luke didn't enjoy reading, he was terrible at spelling and found writing hard work. Yet today he's an author! When not writing, Luke spends most of his time visiting schools and bringing his stories to life with the children he meets.

WWW.LuKeteMPLe.co.UK

Luke's books For KS1

Albert and the Blubber Monster
Albert and the Giant Squid

Luke's books For KS2

The 'Felix Dashwood' series:
Felix Dashwood and the Traitor's Treasure
Felix Dashwood and the Mutating Mansion
Felix Dashwood and the Traitor's Revenge

The 'Ghost Island' series:
Ghost Post
Doorway To Danger
The Ghost Lord Returns

ALBERT AND THE BLUBBER MONSTER

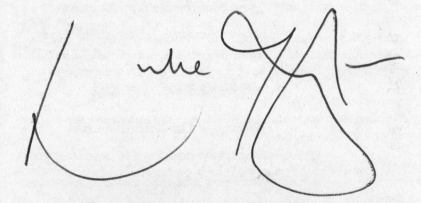

LUKE TEMPLE
ILLUSTRATED BY JESSICA CHIBA

Gull Rock Publications

Dedicated to Margaret and Roy,
with special thanks for all your support over the years!

With thanks to Jessica Chiba, Catherine Coe, Gareth Collinson and
Mike and Barbara Temple

WWW.LUKeteMPLe.co.uK

First published in Great Britain by Gull Rock Publications

The paper used in the printing of this book has been made from wood grown in managed, sustainable forests.

ISBN: 978-0-9572952-5-4

Printed and bound by CPI Group (UK) Ltd, Croydon, CR0 4YY

A catalogue record of this book is available from the British Library

Chapter One: The Bottle

The boat bobbed up and down in the middle of the sea. Well, not quite the middle. Albert could still see Thistlewick Island behind him. He had promised Granddad he wouldn't sail too far away from home.

Albert was out fishing with his best friend, Ernie. There were two cod in Ernie's bucket, but five in Albert's — including one the size of his head!

He was using the new rod Granddad gave him for his seventh birthday yesterday.

Granddad had been a fisherman all his life. With a bald head and long white beard, he looked ancient, but he still told stories about when he was young.

"Once, when I were your age," Granddad had told Albert yesterday as he opened his presents, "I were out fishing when something amazing flew over my boat and into the water."

"Was it a bird?" Albert had asked.

"I thought so at first, but when it popped back out of the water I saw it clearly. It were a merperson."

Albert's mouth had fallen open. "A merperson! A real one?"

Granddad had nodded. "A young mermaid, with black hair and a bright blue tail. She grinned at me, jumped over my boat again and swam off. Of course, no one back on Thistlewick believed me."

"I believe you, Granddad! Do you think I'll ever meet a mermaid?"

"Who knows, Albie. Keep your eyes open and you could see many wonderful things out at sea."

Albert stared at his fishing rod now, wondering what stories he would have to tell by the time he was ancient like Granddad.

Something tugged on his rod and Albert quickly wound the handle. Ernie watched too as the fishing line rose out of the water. How big would this fish be?

"Oh…"

There was no fish.
Albert had caught a
bottle, covered
in seaweed.
He frowned
as he peeled
the slimy green
stuff off.

"Can you
see anything inside it?" asked Ernie.

"Some paper." Albert's heart started
to thump as he read the curly writing
on it: "It says, 'Help me!'"

CHAPTER TWO:
FOLLOW THE GLOW

Ernie stared at the bottle. "Glow? What glow?"

The bottle seemed to answer Ernie's question – it began to glow bright gold!

"Wow!" said Albert. "Come on, let's follow it!"

"I ... I'm not sure. You promised your granddad we wouldn't sail far from Thistlewick."

"But whoever sent this needs help."

Ernie sighed. "Fine. But how can a glow show us where to go?"

Once again, the bottle seemed to understand. The glow inside it formed an arrow shape, pointing left.

Albert and Ernie started to row, following the arrow. The bottle told them to sail east, then south, then east again.

All Albert could see around them now was sea. Butterflies of excitement fluttered around his stomach – he had never been this far away from Thistlewick.

Albert noticed Ernie staring upwards. "There's a storm coming, Albie."

Sure enough, the sky darkened and giant drops

of rain plopped down into the boat.

The waves around them grew larger, and the boat started to rock.

Ernie's eyes darted around nervously. "We should go home."

Albert was about to agree when he spotted a hard rocky surface right ahead, where the arrow pointed.

"Look, Ern, look!"

They tied up the boat and clambered onto the rock. The sky cleared to reveal a whole

rock-covered

island in front

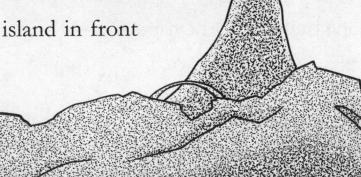

of them. At the centre of it a thin, grey hill rose up.

"This is weird," said Ernie. "It's like Thistlewick, but with no grass or trees or houses. No one could live here."

"But the arrow definitely pointed here." Albert held the bottle up and the arrow inside pointed right. "Let's keep following it!"

They carefully walked over the hard, slippery rock. The bottle was taking them closer to the grey hill. Now Albert thought he could make out a stone building at the top of it.

Near the bottom of the hill they came across a large bridge made of rough stone, like a grey rainbow towering over them. The arrow pointed right at it, so they walked under it into shadow.

"Whoa!" Ernie gasped.

"What is it?"

Albert held the bottle out to get a better look and saw the beak of a dolphin next to Ernie's face.

"That's just a statue, Ern."

"But … it's floating!"

Albert shone the bottle around the dolphin – Ernie was right, it hung in mid-air. "How can a statue float?"

"Look, there's more of them," said Ernie, pointing to ten more grey floating statues lined up alongside the first one.

"A whole pod of dolphins!"

The bottle glowed even harder, pointing through the bridge to the other side.

In the distance, Albert noticed a different colour – a patch of emerald blue standing out against the grey rock.

"Come on, Ern."

They moved towards it.

"It's a rock pool," said Ernie, as they reached the edge.

Albert frowned. "This has to be where the bottle wanted us to come. But there's no one here."

Ernie pointed at the pool. "Wait — what's that? Is it a real dolphin?"

Albert stared into the rippling water. A bright blue forked tail suddenly lifted up.

"That's not a dolphin. It's got scales. It's a giant fish!"

The creature's tail splashed back into the water and its top half appeared. They both gasped at the sight.

A young girl with a round face and

long black hair stared at them, her
eyebrows raised.

"Who are you?" she asked in a shaky
voice.

Chapter Three:
Elody

"I-I'm Albert a-and this is Ernie," Albert stuttered. "Who are you?"

"My … my name is Elody."

"Did you send this?" Albert held out the bottle.

Elody frowned at it, then her amber eyes lit up. "My bottle! Of course! That's why you're here."

She swam closer to them.

"The bottle said you needed help," said Albert. "So we followed the glow."

"Oh … yes. But, you see, I sent the bottle seventy years ago."

"Seventy years!" Ernie's mouth fell opened.

"That can't be right," said Albert. "You look the same age as us!"

"That's because I'm a merperson — we don't ever look old. But I am one hundred and seven."

Now Albert's mouth gaped open like

Ernie's. They were talking to a mermaid who was over a hundred years old!

"No one lives that long, do they?" asked Ernie.

"Mermaids are immortal," Elody explained. "We can live forever."

"Wow!"

Was this the mermaid that his granddad had seen all those years ago, Albert wondered?

"Can we still help you?" he asked.

Elody sighed. "I hope so! I need help against the Blubber Monster, you see."

Albert and Ernie looked at each other. They didn't like the sound of that…

Chapter Four:
The Blubber Monster

"What is the Blubber Monster?" asked Ernie.

"A fish-person," Elody replied in a whisper, like it was dangerous to talk about. "That's what merpeople turn into if we do something bad. Everything switches around. You grow the body of a human and the head of a fish and are forced to live above water – on land!"

"So it's a punishment?" asked Albert.

Elody nodded. "Before I was born, the Blubber Monster stole a magical necklace from a human king, King Honeybone. Because we're not meant to be seen by humans, stealing from them is a big crime. The Blubber Monster changed into a fish-person right there and then, but when he put the necklace on, its magic made him huge and powerful. King Honeybone sent an army of soldiers after him to get the necklace back. The Blubber Monster ran through lots of human towns and villages, crushing houses as he tried to find somewhere to hide from the army."

"Did he come here?" said Albert. "Is that why you need help?"

"Let me show you…"

Elody's tail lifted up and flicked the water, making it ripple. In the ripple, an image appeared, showing Elody in the same place she was now, but the island was underwater. It was really colourful too – full of reds, greens and golds. In the distance was the bridge, and under it dolphins were playing.

"I was relaxing at my favourite spot here on Shelldrake Island – the plughole," Elody explained. "Warm bubbles used to come up through the plughole and tickle me."

In the image, an older merman with a tense face swam up to her.

"What's the matter, Dad?"

"The Blubber Monster is here, Elody!"

Behind Elody and her dad a blurry mass appeared. Albert squinted – it looked like a gigantic, fat, green person.

Elody screamed and her dad

hugged her tightly. But the monster didn't come for them. It plucked something purple and shiny from a nearby rock in its huge hands, roared with laughter then swam out of sight.

"The merstone!" Elody cried. "He's stolen it!"

Her dad's face turned red with anger. "Stay here, Elody – I've got to get the merstone back!"

"Don't leave me, Dad!"

"Be brave, Elody. I will be back soon."

He flicked his tail and swam quickly away. The image faded in the rock pool as he did so.

Albert looked back at Elody and

noticed tears filling her eyes.

"The rock around me started to shake," she said, wiping the tear away. "The merstone had been protecting us – that's its job, to protect its holder – but as soon as the Blubber Monster took it, the stone changed the whole island to protect *him*. He must have planned it – to stay safe from King Honeybone's army."

"The Blubber Monster sounds terrible," said Albert. "What happened to you next?"

"As everything kept shaking, I closed my eyes and stayed in the plughole, like Dad said. When it finally calmed down, I swam up and poked my head out, and there was sky above me. My home had risen above the water. It had changed colour too – all the beautiful reds and greens were now grey. Then I saw my dolphins over by the bridge. They were grey too – they had turned to stone!"

"We saw your dolphins. Why did they turn to stone?" asked Albert.

"Dad always told me that if we magical ocean creatures spend too much time out of water, we turn to stone. I used to think he made it up so that I didn't go too far from home, but now I know it's true."

"What happened to your dad?" asked

Ernie. "And where did the Blubber Monster take the merstone?"

Elody looked up at the hill at the centre of the island. "The castle up there used to be our home. I saw Dad chasing the Blubber Monster into it.

I hoped and hoped he would return, but he never did. He probably turned to stone too – or worse!"

"And if you'd gone after him that would have happened to you too," Albert realised. "So you sent the bottle asking for help."

Elody nodded. Tears streamed down her face. "After seventy years, I had given up hope. But then you two arrived."

Albert squinted up at the hill and recognised the building on top now as a castle. He knew what he had to do.

He turned back to Elody. "Ernie and me will go up there. We'll find out what happened to your dad and merstone."

Chapter Five:
Blubber
Castle

Albert and Ernie were panting heavily when they got to the top of the grey hill. The climb had been very steep.

Ernie's eyes widened. "Whoa! That's a huge castle!"

Many turrets of thick grey stone towered into the sky around the castle. At the centre of it was a tall metal gate. In front of this stood two guards in suits of armour. Albert stared at them: their bodies were human-shaped, but their heads were shark-like. One head was pointed, like a bullet with eyes and a mouth, and the other was the shape of a hammer-head.

"They're fish-people," Albert realised.

"Quick – hide!" Ernie whispered, crouching behind a rock. "Remember what Elody said? The Blubber Monster thinks King Honeybone's army is still after him. He hates humans."

Albert joined him. "How can we get past them?"

"We can't. They have swords. It's too dangerous."

"Those suits of armour look heavy. We could outrun them easily."

"Too risky." Ernie paused. "But the Blubber Monster loves treasure, doesn't he… I've got an idea. Put your coat over your head."

"Why?"

"We're going to pretend to be fish-people!"

Ernie lifted his coat up so his head couldn't be seen. He stood up and walked towards the castle gate.

Albert frowned, but followed. What was Ernie playing at?

"Oi!" called Bullet-head. He snarled at them.

Peeking through a gap in his coat, Albert saw the guard's razor-sharp teeth.

"Who are you? How did you find Blubber Castle?" asked Hammer-head.

"We're fish-people, like you," Ernie replied.

"Why are you hiding your heads?" asked Bullet-head.

"We … we've only just turned into fish-people," said Albert. "We look really ugly."

Hammer-head nodded and his voice softened. "You'll get used to it. But why are you here? We're Lord Blubber's guards — he doesn't need any more."

"We don't want to be guards. We have

brought Lord Blubber some treasure," Ernie replied.

Albert narrowed his eyes. *What treasure?*

Ernie looked at Albert and mouthed, "The bottle."

Suddenly Albert realised: Ernie wanted to trick the guards into thinking the bottle was treasure.

Albert stepped towards them and held the bottle out, hoping it would glow again – then it really would look like treasure.

The guards towered above him, over two metres high, the size of real sharks. Hammer-head's armour creaked as he

bent down to look at the bottle, which
glowed brighter than ever.

"It's so shiiiiiny," said Hammer-head.
"What does it do?"

Albert thought fast. "It grants three
wishes."

"Oooooh." Bullet-head gave him
a toothy grin. "That's one wish for

Lord Blubber and one for each of us. What will you wish for, Hammy?"

"Hmmm … I've always dreamed of being a ballerina," said Hammer-head. "I once stole a tutu from a princess. I think it suited me. What about you?"

"I've always wanted to be called Bob. I hate my real name."

"Oh, but I think Pointy-pointy-nose suits you!" said Hammer-head.

Under his coat, Albert smiled.

Ernie coughed. "So can we go in?"

"Oh, right, yes," said Bullet-head. "I will take you both to meet Lord Blubber."

Chapter Six:
Lord Blubber

They followed Bullet-head along a wide stone corridor.

Ernie pointed at something to their right as they walked. Albert looked over and saw a grey statue with the tail of a fish and the top half of a human. It was pressed against the wall, its eyes wide with fear.

"That's Elody's dad," Albert hissed. "He must have been cornered by Lord Blubber when he turned to stone."

"Do you think he'll change back if he goes in water again?" Ernie whispered.

"I'm not sure. The only way we'll know is if we get the merstone back—"

Bullet-head turned around then. "Hurry up, you two."

The boys rushed to catch the guard up. Albert took in more of their surroundings. Half of the wooden doors were normal-sized, but half were gigantic, at least ten times his height. Bullet-head stopped at one of the giant doors and knocked.

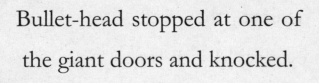

"Enter!" a voice thundered.

The door opened by itself and bright light flooded in through the gaps in Albert's coat. They walked into a large chamber.

Albert gasped at he took in the huge mass sitting at the other end.

The Blubber Monster was far uglier than Albert had imagined, as wide as he was tall. He looked like a humungous trod-on beach ball,

with wrinkles creasing his greenish-grey skin. On top of his swollen blob of a head sat a pearl-covered crown. Around Lord Blubber's neck was a necklace, shimmering against the sickly skin. It must be the one he had stolen from King Honeybone.

If the monster kept the necklace so close, the merstone must be somewhere on him too. Albert looked, but couldn't see it anywhere.

"Who are you? Why are you hiding your heads?" Lord Blubber boomed, making the whole room shake.

"We have some treasure for you," said Albert, hoping that the mention of treasure would distract the monster from their odd appearance.

"What?"

"A golden bottle that grants wishes."

"I've seen it, Lord Blubber," said Bullet-head. "It's shiiiiiny."

The monster's eyes widened. He licked his fat lips. "Come forwards. Show me!"

Albert did as he was told, careful to keep his coat wrapped around his head. As he got nearer he saw just how huge Lord Blubber was. He could crush Albert with his little finger if he wanted to.

The Blubber Monster reached down and, with two fingertips, pulled the bottle out of Albert's hand. It glowed brightly as he held it up to his face.

"Bottle, stop King Honeybone's army from searching for me. Make King Honeybone forget about the necklace!"

"Lord Blubber," said Bullet-head. "You're … you're not going to use up all the wishes, are you? I was hoping I could use one…"

"Silence!" The monster waited. Nothing happened. He grunted. "How do I know if it has worked?"

"It will only work if you give something of your own away," said Ernie.

Albert realised what Ernie was trying to do – get the monster to give them the merstone.

"I see…" Lord Blubber sat back. He sniffed, and frowned. Then he sniffed again. "You two don't smell like fish-people. And why are you hiding? You didn't answer me the first time."

He reached towards Albert. Before Albert could move away, the monster pulled down his coat with a fingernail.

"Humans!" he roared. "How did you find me? No human can find my island! This is a trick, isn't it? King Honeybone sent you to trick me!"

Large globules of spit landed on Albert's face, but he couldn't wipe them off. He was frozen in fear.

"What is in this bottle? It's poison,

isn't it? You were trying to poison me!"

Lord Blubber swung his tree-trunk-sized arm and hurled the bottle across the room. It smashed against the opposite wall.

Albert's heart stopped as the slimy monster's large hand reached towards him and picked him up.

"Albie!" Ernie cried. He ran forwards, but the guard grabbed hold of him.

Is Lord Blubber going to throw me too? Albert thought, dangling many metres off the ground. It would break every bone in his body. He thrashed his legs in panic.

"WHAT ARE YOU DOING IN MY

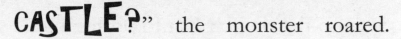

CASTLE?" the monster roared.

"We … we were just out fishing and … got lost!" cried Albert.

That was when he looked at the lumpy fingers squeezing him.

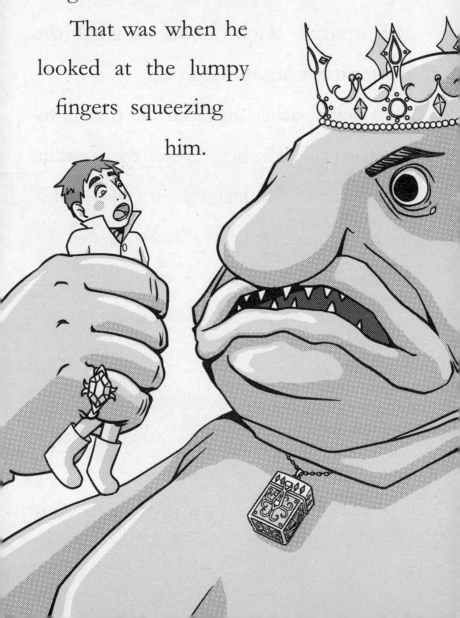

Set into the ring on Lord Blubber's little finger was a purple diamond.

The merstone!

But before Albert could do anything, the monster put him down.

"Guard, take these human rats to my torture chamber. Show them what happened to the last human who came here!"

Chapter Seven:
The Key

Albert and Ernie were locked in a cage high above the ground. Hanging next to it was a small boat with a skeleton sitting inside, a fishing rod grasped between its bony fingers.

Ernie looked at it, his face as white as chalk. "That's what Lord Blubber does to humans."

"Don't worry, Ern, we'll find a way to get out." But as Albert said it, he realised he didn't have a clue how.

"Oi! Quit talking up there," Bullet -head called from the chair he was slouched on below. "Lord Blubber is sleeping. You'd better not wake him, unless you want your heads ripping off."

"Sorry, Pointy-pointy-nose," said Albert.

The boys fell silent.

Time dragged by, but it gave Albert the chance to think of a plan.

He eyed up the skeleton's fishing rod and the key hanging on a hook next to Bullet-head. He just needed the guard to fall asleep.

***

Hours later, Albert finally saw Bullet-head's eyes close and his head drop.

"Ern, you've got skinny arms," Albert whispered. "Can you reach through the bars of our cage and grab the skeleton's fishing rod?"

Ernie frowned, but slid his arm

between the bars. He reached over, having to press himself right against the bars to touch the skeleton's hand. He flinched.

"Keep going!" Albert whispered.

Ernie grabbed the fishing rod. It came away easily, but so did one of the skeleton's fingers. The finger flew out of the boat and clattered to the floor below.

Albert grimaced. Bullet-head turned towards the noise, but his eyes were still shut.

Ernie pulled the fishing rod into the cage. "Here you go."

"Great work, Ern!"

Albert took the rod. He swung the

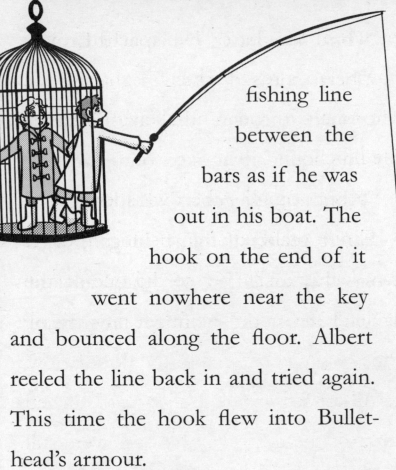

fishing line between the bars as if he was out in his boat. The hook on the end of it went nowhere near the key and bounced along the floor. Albert reeled the line back in and tried again. This time the hook flew into Bullet-head's armour.

CLANG!

Bullet-head simply grunted and continued sleeping.

"Third time lucky," whispered Ernie.

Albert released the line again. It whooshed through the air. With a jangling sound it hooked onto the key.

"I think you've got it!" said Ernie.

Albert reeled the line in and, with a tug, the key lifted off the wall and dangled across the room towards them.

Chapter Eight:
Lord Blubber's Bedroom

Their footsteps echoed around the castle as they ran, looking left and right for Lord Blubber.

"Where is he?" Ernie panted.

A loud rumbling echoed down the corridor. A few seconds later, another rumble followed.

Albert grinned. "That's him snoring. Follow that noise!"

The snoring was coming from behind a huge wooden door. With all their strength they heaved it open. The full force of the sound hit them, rattling through their bodies.

SNOOOOORE!

Ahead was a gigantic bed, almost twice their height.

"Lift me up, Ern."

Albert climbed onto Ernie's shoulders. He gripped the edge of the bed and pulled himself up onto the

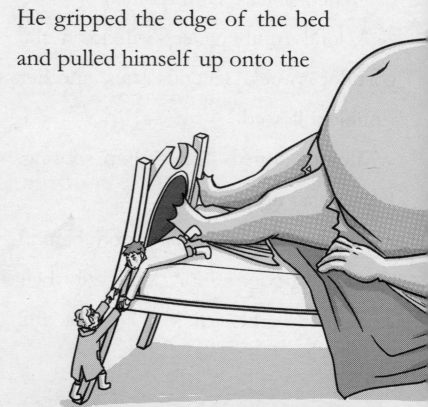

squidgy mattress. In front of him was the sickly-green mass of Lord Blubber.

Albert leant over the side, grabbed Ernie's hands and pulled him up.

"There it is." Albert pointed to the ring on the monster's little finger, with the shiny purple merstone. "I hope he's a deep sleeper."

SNOOOOOORE!

Albert climbed over to the monster's hand and sat on it.

"I'll hold his finger down. You pull the ring off," he told Ernie.

SNOOOOORE!

Ernie's hands shook as they hovered over Lord Blubber's huge finger. He grasped the ring and tugged it.

"It's not budging," he mouthed.

"Keep trying!" Albert whispered.

Ernie did, but the monster's finger was too blubbery and the ring got stuck in between rolls of fat.

GRUNT!

Ernie jumped back at the sound but

Albert didn't have a chance – he was being lifted up! He clung onto Lord Blubber's finger as it swung into the air. The monster had woken up!

He was about to shout to Ernie to run, when he saw that the monster's eyes were firmly shut. He was still asleep!

Albert held on tightly as Lord Blubber's hand travelled up to his face. The top of the monster's little finger disappeared deep inside his nose.

Eurgh! thought Albert, holding onto the finger, which began to drip with gooey green liquid.

Lord Blubber gave a satisfied snort and lowered his arm to the bed. Albert jumped off, wiped at his face and felt the snot smear all over him.

"Gross! Monster bogeys!"

"They're all over you. And the ring." Ernie screwed up his face.

The liquid plopped off the monster's finger and formed a puddle on the bed.

"Come on, we have to get the ring," said Albert.

"I'm not touching that."

"Ern, it's just a bit of snot."

Ernie stepped forwards slowly, staring

at the ring. His left foot slipped in the snot puddle. Splat! He landed right in it.

"Yuuuuuck!" Ernie yelled, forgetting about keeping quiet.

Albert leant down and helped Ernie up. Ernie's face glistened with goo. He looked like he was about to be sick.

Ernie puffed out his cheeks. "OK, so now I'm covered too. Let's get on with this."

Together they grabbed hold of the ring and heaved. Lord Blubber's snot squelched around Albert's hands, but the disgusting liquid made it much easier to pull. They staggered back, grinning, as the ring came off the monster's finger.

Chapter Nine:
The Chase

Albert and Ernie rushed out through the castle gates. Hammer-head clunked along behind them, but couldn't keep up.

"You two! Come here!"

"Do you think the Blubber Monster's still asleep?" said Albert.

He was answered by a

ROAAAAAR!

"Um, not now!" said Ernie.

"Run!" Albert cried.

They fled as fast as they could down the grey hill.

"What do we do?" asked
Ernie.

"Get the merstone to
Elody. She'll know
what to do with it."

THUD!

The ground under them shook.

"He's out of the castle!" Ernie realised. "Quick!"

They put their heads down and charged ahead.

THUD! STOMP!

"Oh, humans! I'm coming for YOU!" came the monster's voice as they reached the bridge at the bottom of the hill.

STOMP! THUD!

Albert looked back and saw the giant figure halfway down the hill. He was just a few stomps away.

Lord Blubber's arms swung in the air and he let out another huge

ROAAAAAAAR!

Albert thrust the merstone into Ernie's hand. "You take it to Elody in her plughole. I'll try to distract Lord Blubber."

Ernie's eyebrows rose uncertainly, but he nodded and ran.

Albert watched Ernie go, then looked around for something to help him. His eyes landed on the bridge – it must be even taller than the monster.

I can take him by surprise.

Albert grabbed the rough stone

of the bridge and pulled his feet up, getting to the top just as Lord Blubber approached. He ducked down so the monster couldn't see him.

"Oh, humans! I can smell **YOU!**"

Albert shut his mouth, not daring to breathe. The monster disappeared under the bridge and Albert ran across to the other side.

Albert leapt from the bridge just as Lord Blubber emerged. He fell onto the monster's shoulders and grabbed at something to hold onto. His hands landed on the necklace.

The necklace! Albert had an idea.

"Ah! There you are, boy!" Lord

Blubber reached up a fat arm. "What are you doing? No! Get off my necklace!"

"It's not yours. It's King Honeybone's."

"I knew you were working for *him*!"

The monster flung his arms in the air and spun around and around, shaking Albert about wildly.

The metal of the necklace cut painfully into his hands but he refused to let go. He felt along the necklace and finally found what he was looking for — the catch that held it together.

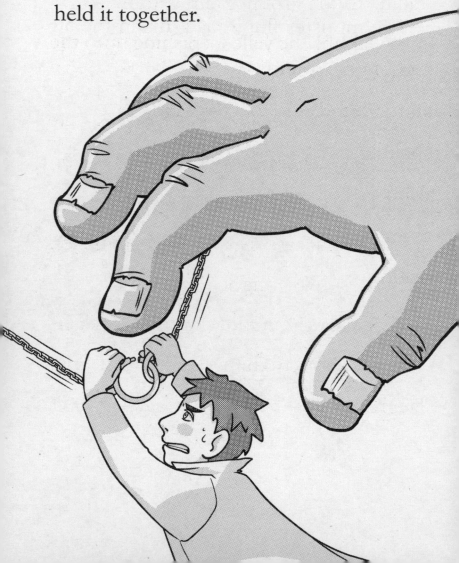

He pushed it firmly.

SNAP!

Albert felt the necklace break in two –
falling to the ground, him with it.

"Aaahhh!" he yelled, crashing onto the
rock.

Shaking the pain off, Albert quickly
rolled over to look for Lord Blubber.
He saw the large necklace lying on the
ground, but no sign of the monster.
Where had he gone?

Then, in the middle of the necklace,
Albert spotted him, and burst out
laughing.

Chapter Ten:
The Whirlpool

Albert found Ernie by the plughole, with Elody floating in the water. Ernie had just given her the merstone.

"Albert!"

"Where is Lord Blubber?" asked Elody. "Is that his ecklace?"

Albert nodded. "Look."

The jewel on the necklace was a box pendant covered in gems. Albert pressed a button and it clicked open.

Ernie's eyes widened. "Is that…?"

"Yep!" Albert grinned. "I've put him

in here so he doesn't cause any more trouble."

Standing in the box, just ten centimetres tall, was Lord Blubber. He shook a fist at Albert and squeaked, "Give me back my merstone!"

"It's not your merstone," Albert replied, and shut the box.

"How…?" Elody began.

"The necklace is magical, remember It's what made the

Blubber Monster powerful, and it obviously made him a hundred times bigger than he was. Without it he's more of a Blubber Mouse!"

A huge smile spread over Elody's face and she spun around excitedly. "Well done, Albert. Thank you!"

"So where does the merstone go?" he asked.

"Just in this rock here."

Elody swam over to it — the same rock she had clung to when Albert and Ernie had first met her. She lifted the merstone up and pushed it right into the rock. Suddenly the whole rock glowed purple.

"Whoa!" cried Ernie.

Elody smiled, then disappeared below the water.

The ground under their feet shook then, like when Lord Blubber had chased them but ten times worse. Albert looked uncertainly at Ernie.

With a fierce roar, water gushed out of the plughole, flooding around their feet.

"It's working. The island's going back below the sea."

"But we're going down with it!" cried Ernie.

Albert gripped Ernie's arm, but it was no good. Their feet swept from under them and they fell into the rushing water, spinning round and round. The boys thrashed their arms and legs, but they couldn't stop the plughole sucking them down. Albert grew sick with dizziness as the world around him got darker and darker until it turned black.

Chapter Eleven:
The Dolphin Chariot

Albert opened his eyes and gasped for air.

He frowned at the sight of seaweed and bubbles in the water around him. He was deep underwater. How was he able to breathe?

Then he saw Ernie next to him, head inside a large glass ball, like an upside-down fish bowl. Albert realised he must be wearing one too.

A figure with a bright blue tail floated up to them. Elody!

"You're awake!" She swam over and gave them each a hug. "You did it! You saved Shelldrake Island from the Blubber Monster! Look!"

Albert blinked and stared around. He almost didn't recognise the island. Above the water it had been grey, but underwater it was so colourful – a patchwork of greens and reds. He saw the hill above them. The castle on top of it shone a brilliant gold. It was amazing!

"What about your dad?" asked Albert. "And the dolphins?"

A large merman appeared next to Elody then, his tail bright green. "We came back to life again, as soon as the water hit us."

"Albert, Ernie, meet my dad!" said Elody.

"Call me Erlyn. Elody has told me

what you both did. With all my heart, I thank you." Erlyn's voice was deep and warm. "I have locked the Blubber Monster and his guards in our castle dungeon."

Albert felt something soft pushing against his back. He turned to see the beak of a dolphin nuzzling him.

"Hello," he said.

The dolphin squeaked back happily. Several more appeared. Their tails splashed through the water as they danced around the boys and blew bubbles at each other.

Erlyn let out a hearty laugh, and the three children were soon giggling too.

To say thank you, Elody and Erlyn offered to take Albert and Ernie back home in their golden chariot.

"No human has ever been allowed in it before," Erlyn explained.

Eleven dolphins pulled the chariot up out of the water and into sunlight. Albert and Ernie took off their glass balls and breathed fresh air.

"Look, it's my boat!" Albert pointed to it floating nearby.

They tied his boat to the chariot, then Erlyn called, "Hold on tight! Dolphins, off we go!"

The dolphins squeaked and leapt into action, the chariot dancing along behind them. Erlyn stood at the front, pulling the reins and guiding the dolphins left and right. They got faster, their tails splashing excitedly through the water. Albert and Ernie whooped and cheered as the chariot bounced over waves.

In no time at all, they had arrived at Thistlewick and Albert and Ernie stepped back into the harbour.

"Thank you again," said Erlyn, untying Albert's boat. "And do not forget, you are always welcome at Shelldrake Island."

"Can I come to Thistlewick to see Albert and Ernie as well, Dad?" asked Elody.

"We are not supposed to be seen by humans, Elody." A smile formed on his face. "But Albert and Ernie have been very kind to us. As long as you are careful not to be seen by anyone else, then yes, you may."

Albert beamed at Elody. "See you soon, then."

A tear ran down her cheek. She smiled back at him. "Very soon."

"Right, we must return King Honeybone's necklace." Erlyn winked at the boys, then said, "Dolphins, let's go!"

Albert and Ernie watched the chariot ride away across the water. It glowed magically in the golden sunlight. The dolphins pulled the chariot over a tall wave and disappeared behind it.

There was a tap on Albert's shoulder. He turned to see Granddad standing there, his wrinkles creased into a frown.

"I've been worried sick. I told you not to sail too far out."

"Sorry," said Ernie.

"Sorry, Granddad," said Albert.

"Where on earth have you been?"

"You'll never believe us, Granddad, but look." Albert pointed out to sea, but the chariot was gone. "Oh… Well, you'll just have to believe me. We met a mermaid – I think it's the same mermaid you saw!"

"She's called Elody," said Ernie.

For a while, Granddad didn't say anything. His bushy eyebrows knitted together in a quizzical look.

Finally, he said, "I believe you."

"You do?" asked Albert.

Granddad nodded. "I am always telling you stories, Albie, and now you have one for me. Let's go and have some tea. You two can tell me all about it."

They walked up the path away from the harbour.

Albert smiled as he thought of Elody, about saving Shelldrake Island, and of the adventures that might be just around the corner…

AN iNterVieW WiTH LuKe TeMPLe

QueStiON: *Who is your favourite character in* Albert and the Blubber Monster?

ANSWer: I love the two guards, Hammer-head and Bullet-head. They would be quite scary if they weren't so silly.

Q: Which is your favourite chapter in the book?

Turn over to read LuKe'S ANSWer!

A: Definitely chapter 8, in Lord Blubber's bedroom. I tried to make it as disgusting as possible!

Q: How long did it take you to write the book?

A: It took me 6 months to write. I didn't spend all that time actually writing, though. Most of the time I was just letting ideas build up in my head.

Q: What is the worst thing you have ever written?

A: I once tried to write a book about Albert turning into a talking fish. I got about half way through, then realised that it was a very silly idea.

Q: If you turned into a fish, what fish would you want to be?

A: I'd like to be a puffer fish. Or a blob fish. Or a fish finger.

Q: What is your favourite word?

A: 'Syzygy' – because no one ever guesses how to spell it.

Q: Have you always wanted to be an author?

A: No. When I was a child I wanted to be a zookeeper. Then I found out that zookeepers have to clean up all the animal poo, so I decided I didn't like that idea!

Q: What books did you read when you were a child?

A: I found reading really hard as a child, so I didn't read many books!

I loved listening to people reading stories to me, though. My favourites were the 'Noddy' stories.

AN iNterVieW WiTH iLLUStrator Jessica CHiba

QueStiON: How did you decide what Albert and Ernie would look like?

ANSWer: Albert is a confident and active boy, so I gave him strong eyebrows and scruffy hair. I wanted Ernie to have curly hair, to be different from Albert. I also thought it suited his personality more. They wear fishing coats, because nobody wants to get fishy smells on nice clothes!

Q: What about Elody and the Blubber Monster?

A: I wanted Elody to look beautiful. She has big, curly hair that floats in water, and there are lots of pearls hanging in her curls.

The Blubber Monster is based on the blob fish. He needed to be ugly, and the blob fish is perfect because it was voted the world's ugliest animal. It's the official mascot of the Ugly Animal Preservation Society!

Q: Which was your favourite illustration to draw?

A: Albert and Ernie covered in snot! I thought it was a disgusting idea, so I wasn't looking forward to drawing it. But I actually really enjoyed doing all the goo and drawing Albert and Ernie's expressions of disgust.

Q: What is your favourite thing to draw?

A: People, because they can have such funny expressions! I also really enjoy drawing fantasy creatures, so drawing mermaids and mermen was a treat!

Q: If you were a fish, what fish would you be?

A: Ooh, difficult question! I like to think I would be an octopus or a starfish.

Here are some of Jessica's very first sketches of the characters!

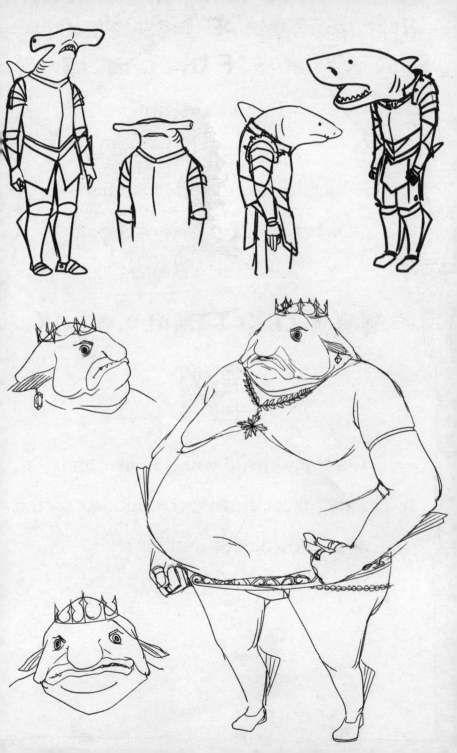

To find out more
about how Luke and
Jessica wrote and illustrated
Albert and the Blubber Monster
visit the website:

WWW.LUKeteMPLe.CO.UK

On the website you can also find:
fascinating facts, fun videos, hidden secrets,
downloads and more!

knock
knock